A DONKEY FOR NESSA

SUZAN JANET

CONTENTS

CHAPTER ONE

It's Time

She held her breath. She was afraid that even her breathing would put her in danger. The hairs on her head stood like soldiers at attention from the adrenaline rushing through her veins. She waited for the next lightning strike so she could see what she feared.

The rain had been falling lightly when she went to bed and the constant patter on the roof had lulled her to sleep quickly but now she was wide awake. The lightning that had awaken her, illuminated that which had her frozen like museum statue. Her chest began to feel tight. She knew the urge to take a breath would soon overcome. "Come on lightning." She thought anxiously. Just then the sky began to rumble and "Crack" the sky lit up her room and there it was.

At the end of her bed, upon the blanket, where her feet lay frozen beneath was a spider the size of a watermelon. She couldn't just lay there. She slowly moved her hands to the edges of the blanket and in one move she lifted the blanket and cracked it down like a whip in an attempt to flip the spider off the bed.

She let go of the blanket, rolled off the bed, ran toward the door and grabbed the knob. Nothing. It wouldn't move. Both hands now on the knob, she twisted, pulled, and kicked the door and still nothing.

The room was now so black she couldn't see her hands on the door. Just then, another lightning strike lit up her room, she twirled around to see if the spider was trapped within the blanket. She let out an ear piercing scream as the gigantic black arachnid sprung from its shinny pointed legs directly at her head.

Nessa woke up with her blanket tangled around her feet. Her heart pounding a rhythm sufficient for a techno dance party. All a nightmare. She kicked off the blanket and settled back into her bed. Taking slow deep breaths to eliminate the uneasy thought of the dream that felt so real. Finally, in a state of relaxation and near entry back into the dream world, Nessa remembered.

It was a special day. Time to wake up. She stretched her legs out tight all the way to her toes like a ballerina and raised her arms above her head performing a full body stretch. At 6 years. old she barely covered half the size of her twin bed. Some would see her as a petit fragile doll. Crystal blue eyes against bone white skin that was framed in locks of spun gold. But Nessa was anything but fragile. She had strength beyond her size and a will as strong as monkeys grip on a peanut. Today she would have a chance to show just how strong she could be.

She shook off the nightmare and swung her legs to the floor. Her excitement was almost more than she could bear. The day had finally arrived! "When would everyone else get up?" Nessa thought. "Aren't they as excited as I am to finally move into our new house in the country?" Today was the day she could call herself a country girl. Dreams of planting a garden and having her own pets was about to come true, but not soon enough for Nessa.

She could wait no longer. She popped out of her bed and scurried her socked feet across the room to her sister Jennifer's bed and gave her a couple quick shoves.

Jennifer groaned "HEY STOP". Nessa bent down, close to her ear, and whispered

"Wake up sleepy head! It's moving day; time for county living!"

Hearing the commotion, Ally, her other sister, slowly pulled the covers off of her head, a fist full at a time. She cautiously lifted her heavy eyelids open, slowly preparing to squint from the morning sun.

"It's still dark Nessa" whispered Ally. Nessa was already running down the hall headed toward her little brother Zach's room. She nearly missed his door, as her socks slid, carrying her across the polished wood floors. She managed to grab the door frame, barley navigating the turn in time to fly into his room making the landing onto his bed.

It's time! It's time!" Nessa shouted. He giggled with delight and promptly began jumping up and down on the bed in his footed PJs. Zach, almost 4 years. old, wasn't sure what it was "time" for but anything his sisters wanted, Zach wanted to!

He loved his 3 older sisters and he was smothered with the attention of all three. Jennifer was the first born and a full 2 years later, came Nessa. Their parents Greg and Stephanie, hoping they would have a boy thought "third times a charm". So they had their third child, a daughter named Ally.

Greg, and Stephanie or "Steph" as most family called her, had a house full of girls and loved every minute of it. Yet they still had hopes of having a boy so deciding to even out the numbers they gave it one more shot. And Zach was born 3 years. after Ally. The family seemed complete. Or so they thought.

Steph and Greg could hear the floor above them coming to life. It was a big day and lots of work ahead of them. Moving 4 children and an entire household to a country home was going to be a challenge. They would all need to work together. The saying "Many hands make small work" may be true but if the hands that are working are small they can easily get sidetracked, as Steph and Greg would soon see.

Nessa finally made her way downstairs to her mom and Dad's room where she found them up and brushing their teeth. "Mom, Dad!" Nessa shouted in a feverish pitch, "It's finally here! I can't wait to go climb the trees and plant my garden and buy some chickens and ......Vanessa, Vanessa, Vanessa" Said her Dad, "Slow down. We have lots to do before we can even think about a garden and chickens. All in due time young lady, all in due time."

Her Dad loved the non-stop enthusiasm of their second daughter. And each one of their children gave him a reflection of the best that life had to offer.

Ally could sing like an angel and Zach, even at his young age, was a comedian. Jennifer was a bit more serious and balanced her intellect with her athleticism.

He was a patient and loving father and husband. Sometimes he struggled to balance their, needs from their wants, because he was the kind of Dad that wanted to give them everything. It was often challenging to be there for back to school nights or performances due to Greg's long hours out of town. Some jobs kept him away for weeks at a time. Steph was always able to manage the house just fine while he was gone, which decreased his worry. He always returned to a home filled with the joy and laughter of his family, and so it replenished his soul, making it worth the sacrifice.

Now he wondered how Steph would manage in his absence at their new home". So here he was, on this "Moving day", getting his batteries recharged; the first dose from little Nessa.

He finished brushing his teeth, rinsed his mouth and told Nessa "We have things to pack and boxes to move, not to mention an old yard that will need some tending to before the snow falls." He bent down to the level of his blonde haired burst of energy, put his hands on her shoulders and kissed her warm cheek. He could feel her energy bubbling from her toes to her shoulders like an uneven load of laundry as she shifted her weight from foot to foot. She had obviously forgotten about her morning trip to the bathroom in all her excitement.

"Grandma and Grandpa Hugg will be here with the trailer around 10am.Thats in 4 hours." He told Nessa. As he stood up he continued, "Now you go back upstairs, go to the bathroom and get dressed. Then we'll have some breakfast and get this day started with some nourishment in our bellies!

Now GO!" as he gave her a little love pat on her behind.

Nessa zoomed back up the stairs with the same enthusiasm. She was like a leaf caught in the wind of fall breeze, tumbling and twirling and floating through air.

By 9 am breakfast was done, final dishes packed. The preplanning and packing would help the day go smoother but the items that they needed daily were yet to be put away in boxes. Steph gave each of the kids a "To do" list. Jennifer would be in charge of keeping Zach out of the way and Ally was in charge of the bathroom items. It was Nessa's job to help pack the girls' clothes in the boxes.

Everyone must have been focused intently on their tasks because Steph suddenly noticed an unfamiliar sound in the house. A sound she rarely hears, on days that the children are not in school. It was dead quiet! In that moment it hit her. They would be leaving the home where they had been newlyweds, had their first baby, where she cooked their first turkey, raised their first dog and buried Nessa's first pet fish. Yes, buried. It was a full funeral with music and flowers. Nessa insisted. Steph looked around the near empty house and could still feel love that had been shared there.

Just then Greg walked in and saw her standing there. He put his arms around her from behind and said "are you ready for this next adventure?" He felt the moisture of a tear drop on his arm before she could answer. He spun her around and wiped the tears from her face. "I know honey. I know" And he hugged her tight.

CHAPTER TWO

The Move

Ding! Dong; sounded the front door bell. "It must be Grandma and Grandpa" Steph said. The percussion of several feet could be heard descending the stairs sounding like a heard of buffalo "Grandma! Grandpa! "Yelled Ally, Nessa and Jenifer. Gapa! Gama! Squealed Zach. Grandma and Grandpa Hugg had arrived with the trailer and within 3 hours they would have it tightly packed for the last load to the house in the country.

The new home was an old farm house, in need of a lot of tender loving care.

Most young families would have never considered this big of a challenge but Greg and Steph were both hard workers, talented and could approach just about any project as a team. The new property would have plenty of projects with a barn, garage, pasture, and pond. It helped that farm living was not new to Steph. Grandma and Grandpa Hugg had raised her on a farm with a garden, pigs and chickens. Even so, this would be their biggest project yet.

After arriving to the farm with the last load, Steph gave the kids their task list again. She had lots to do and keeping them busy was the best strategy. Jennifer had clothing duty. The boxes were light enough for her to carry up to the girls' rooms. This time Nessa was in charge of Zach and Ally would put the bathroom items away.

Nessa took Zach outside to the barn to see what they could find; maybe the old owners left some chickens. Nessa was curious to see what was inside. She held Zach's hand so tightly with excitement that he winced. When she noticed her vice-like grip she let go." I am a big boy; I can hold my own hand." Zach said. "That's good Zach, cause I think I am going to need both of my hands, to open the barn door." Nessa replied. She took hold of the handle and pulled with her whole body. No movement. Almost 7 years old, Nessa was but a toothpick and her determination was that of an ox. On the third pull she got the door to roll open. While disappointed there were no chickens, she was amazed at the possibilities. She thought to herself," I could have a cow, a horse, a cat, a dog and maybe even a donkey." She imagined them all lined up in the barn. Each would have their very own stall and she would come every morning before school and water and feed them. She would brush their coats, sing to them, and they would love her. She could have a mini circus and teach them tricks. On the week-ends she could put on a show for the neighbors.

Just when she began to think of names for all the animals she would have, she realized Zach was nowhere in sight. She looked around again and called out" Zach"! Nothing. She ran out of the barn. She looked in all directions. No Zach. If she called out to him, Dad might hear her. Then he would know that she lost Zach on her watch. She was a big girl now and if she wanted the responsibility of farm animals she better be able to handle watching her little brother. She didn't want to go into the house because if he was in there then Mom would know she had not done her job. She had to find Zach on her own. In a loud whisper she began calling out". Zach, Zach, Zach". Off to the right of the house was the big road. He couldn't have gotten there so fast. She kept calling for him in a whisper and, as she turned past the corner of the barn, she saw him. She ran in his direction through the pasture. All she could see was his back and head. He was lying on his side. Oh no she thought; hurt on my watch! As she got closer to the base of a big shady Poplar tree, she saw that Zach was not hurt. Not hurt at all. He was curled up, on his side petting a new friend; an old barn cat.

Nessa, relieved, sat down next to him. She leaned her back against the tree trunk and resumed her daydreams of her very own animal circus. As the cat purred, Zach, having been woken way too early that morning, went into his own dreamland.

CHAPTER THREE

Sea Monster

Greg and Steph spent nearly every evening and week-end removing old broken down farm equipment and mowing and trimming the overgrown property. They got lucky with a few items that they were able to salvage and sell for a few dollars. This went into the indoor remodeling fund. There was much to do inside.

July was just around the corner and it was the month for both Ally and Nessa to celebrate their birthday. Because they were born two years and one week apart they had always celebrated their birthdays together. Ally had already mentioned that she would like a pink bicycle but so far there had been no request from Nessa.

Steph had dinner about ready and all the kids were finishing up doing their outside evening chores. Greg had only been home for a few days and would soon be starting a two-week job out of town and so he was out with the kids in the yard. Steph savored the moments when she could get things done without interruption. The quiet of the moment did not last long when she heard the trampling of feet coming toward the front door as though there was no stopping them. She put the last plate down on the table and braced herself against the kitchen wall.

The back door swung open with Jennifer the first to get inside; squealing as she made her way past the kitchen and into the living room. She was followed immediately by a screaming Ally, nearly attached to her was Nessa, and as always, in the rear was Zach. "Shut the door! Shut the door!" yelled Ally. "Don't let Dad in" screamed Jen. It's a monster. Just then Greg flew through the door holding what appeared to the girls as a four-legged green sea monster. This was the biggest bull frog Steph had ever seen. She had spent plenty of days fishing on the river, near her childhood home, using frogs as bait to catch Northerns, but this was like no frog she had ever seen.

The more the girls squealed, the closer Greg carried the green monster into the room. Steph's peace and quiet was now a circus of green legs, tossing pillows and squeals. She decided that both Greg and the kids had had enough excitement for the evening. She walked over to Greg, took hold of the frog and held it like you would a new baby kitten. She cradled one arm below its bottom legs and began to pet the top of its head. "Look at this cute little frog girls, Zach." She went over to the couch and sat down.

Slowly the girls came from behind the couch, where they had sought safety. How could it be a scary monster if Mom was holding it like a baby they though? One by one each of the kids came over and touched the top of the frog's head. "Is it a boy or girl" asked Jennifer. Steph lifted the frog and the kids backed away; afraid another teasing was coming. Even though that was Dads usual move, not Moms, they backed up non the less.

Steph began her amphibian lesson. "Boy bullfrogs are large and have big muscles and when they call out, they have loud deep voices. Like Daddy" Steph said as she turned and smiled at Greg. "You know the sounds we hear at the pond? "Jug a rum- Jug a rum". She mimicked. Girl frogs don't make loud calls like that, just short chirpy sounds or peeps. "Look kids" Steph said as she held it beneath its front legs and turned it so all the kids could see. "See this" as she pointed to a circular area on each side of its mouth, below the eyes. This is a covering over their ears called "tympanic membranes". We have these but they are inside our ears. See how these are much bigger in size than their eyes. In girl frogs, the tympanic membrane is about the same size as the eyes. The boy frog needs bigger ears so they can hear the little chirps and peeps of the girl's voice to find them. And the girl's ears don't have to be that big because the boy is loud! Step elbowed Greg. Another way to tell a boy from a girl is the boy's chin are darkly colored, with a distinctive yellow spotting. The chins of the girl frogs tend to be more yellowish white", Steph finished. "Let's call him "Rum Rum" blurted Zach out of the blue. The girls giggled as Greg and Steph smiled at each other the way parents do when they are tickled by something their child says or does.

After finding a nice sized moving box, as a temporary home, they all washed up and settled to the table for dinner. The topic of conversation became what the girls wanted for their birthdays. Ally had confirmed she indeed wanted a pink bike. Nessa remained quiet. Greg asked once again. Nessa don't you know what you want for your birthday?" "Well, Said Nessa, I do, but I don't think you will get me one." "What is it?" asked Greg? "I want a donkey." She said. The room remained silent. Jennifer and Ally didn't say a word. If Dad wouldn't get her one, they didn't want to encourage her. "Don't you want a bike too?" asked Ally. Then Jennifer thought she had a good idea and suggested "How about a Rainbow bright doll? Nessa looked at her sisters and then back at her Mom and Dad. She slowly lowered her head looking like a dog when he knows he's in trouble." It's OK" Nessa said. "I didn't think you would get me one anyway." Everyone finished eating and went off to play or read. It was noticeable that Nessa's, usually great, appetite was diminished by her disappointment as half her meal remained on the plate.

That evening Greg and Steph discussed her request. They agreed, while odd, it really was no different from a girl asking for a pony. They had plenty of land and already had fencing for larger animals. So, without a good reason to say no, the search was on to find Nessa a Donkey.

CHAPTER FOUR

Life and Death

When Nessa woke, Zach startled her, as his face was inches from hers. He had been waiting for her to wake so they could go visit the sea monster. He was not quite sure it was "OK" to be in the same room alone with the green shiny, bumpy hopper. Nessa pulled her boots on over her pajamas bottoms. She was about to tell Zach to put on his shoes and realized he had been dressed and ready. Well about as dressed as a 3 yr. old. He too had on his pajama bottoms and superman slippers.

They went downstairs and peeked into Mom and Dad's room on their way outside. It was empty. They proceeded around the corner to the kitchen, expecting to see Mom cooking breakfast, and found another empty room. Zach looked at Nessa with his eyebrows lifted like the Mac Donald's golden arches. Without words, Nessa shrugged her shoulders and out the door they went.

The night before, Dad had put the box, housing their green pet, in the barn. Mom and Dad must have gone out there to check on him. As they got closer, they began to hear the familiar pond song of the sea monsters. "Jug-o-rum....Jug-o-rum...Jug-o-rum". Nessa pulled open the barn door and Zach scrambled past her into the barn in search of the box. He looked left and then right and left again as he scanned the barn for what should have been an easy box to spot. "Where is it" wondered Zach out loud. They could no longer hear the call that beckoned when outside the barn. "let's go find Mom and Dad, maybe they moved him to the garage. Before Nessa could move her feet Zach rushed past her. She caught up with him as they reached the garage door.

There was Steph sitting on a bench near their vintage Corvette holding onto some tools while Greg was head deep into the engine. Apparently Greg had not heard them coming because when Zach yelled "where is Rum Rum" his head popped up and hit the hood. Greg rubbed the top of his head as he squinted from the pinch it caused. "Sorry Dad" said Nessa "We just want to know where our frog is at!" While still rubbing the top of his head, Greg squatted down, eye level with Nessa and Zach. "Well kids." He said. I didn't think you would be up so early. I checked on your frog this morning but he was gone when I got there. The box was empty." Zach spun around without a word and was out the garage and in the direction of the barn.

"Where are you going Zach?" hollered Greg. "We heard Rum Rum calling when we walked out this morning. I bet he went back to find him in the barn." Said Nessa. Greg set down the wrench and wiped off his hands on a rag. "Come on Steph, let's go help round up a frog.

When they got to the barn they found Zach crawling under the tack bench. 'Do you see him Zach?" Asked Greg "No but it would be a good hiding spot so I am looking where I would hide if I was a frog.

Nessa walked into the stall where she hoped one day she would have a donkey. As she looked at each corner of the stall she began to daydream of coming into the barn to feed her donkey. This would be where she would brush his coat and feed him carrots. She imagined how he would want to go with her for walks in the pasture; she was so far in her imagination that she could smell the grass that smashed under his feet.

Just then she turned toward the doorway of the stall and with her eyes at the level of the middle rail she was nearly nose to nose with Rum Rum. Startled, she screamed and tried to back up. Steph, Greg and Zach came running into the stall to see Nessa flat on her back with Rum Rum on her chest. "You found him!" Zach said with excitement. Nessa just lay there motionless watching the eyes of a bullfrog staring at her. Up and down went Rum Rum riding her fast paced ribcage like a bronco rider at the rodeo. "Hurry Zach, go ahead and pick him up. Put both hands around him just below his upper legs". Said Steph holding back the laughter that was rising from her belly. Zach hesitated when he reached down toward Rum Rum and in that moment the bull frogs muscular legs and toes pushed off Nessa's chest into the air. Zach dove after him landing half way over Nessa. "Got him" exclaimed Zach as he wiggled onto his knees and held up his capture. "Good job said Greg. Now let's put him back in the box so we can go find a better home for this monster.

Nessa and Steph went back into the house to get some breakfast started while Zach followed his dad like a baby duckling. "What we gona use for his house?" asked Zach continuing to move his little legs briskly to keep up with Greg. "So Zach, frogs need water so I am thinking we can find one of the smaller galvanized water troughs that was left behind the barn when we moved in. Some had some holes in them but we can put a pail in the trough for the frog to get in the water and add some rocks around it. It should be tall enough.

As they neared the back of the barn Greg stopped and turned around. He squatted down to Zach's level and said" Rum Rum will need to be a temporary family member. He can't stay with us for too long Zach. "Why Daddy?" asked Zach. "Well, honey, frogs need other frogs to keep them company. They need to get in water that has bugs to eat and a bigger pond to stretch their legs. But he can visit for a few days." Said Greg.

Zach didn't know what to think. Maybe a few days was a long time he hoped. "I can put my superman blanket in the bucket with him so he won't be scared." Said Zach. Trying not to laugh, Greg replied "Well see Zach.

Over the next hour they located the trough and dragged it to the shady side of the house. They added a bucket full of water and some various rocks from around the yard. Zach picked out most of them and each time he decided on one, he announced "I got one, look dad this one is perfect. Zach pulled some grass from the pasture and added it to Rum Rum's new home.

Greg and Zach went together and got Rum Rum from his temporary box. Zach slowly lowered him into the trough being careful not to fall in behind him. At first the frog sat motionless then slowly hopped the length of the trough and then back the other direction. He seemed to be checking out his new surroundings.

Zach, we still need to get some chicken wire to cover the top because I'm thinking this guy has a good chance of hopping out of his house.

Greg turned toward the shed and Zach followed. They were about half way when Greg heard the screech of a hawk above. He looked up as he always does. The sight of these big birds had always fascinated him. Watching them ride the wind was so calming. He had learned that their eyesight was incredible. They can see a mouse from almost two miles away. He often watched them soar the property, round and round looking for dinner and then suddenly they would dive down to the ground and swoop up their food.

Greg heard the hawk screeched again, he looked up and watched as it went into its downward dive. Greg continued to watch and suddenly he realized the direction it was diving. But it was too late, the hawk had picked up Rum Rum and was at a low climb back into the sky. It seemed to have difficulty getting into the air due to the weight of the frog.

Zack must have seen his frog being taken away by the bird as he began to run in its direction. "Come back here! He is my friend not yours! Let him go! Let him go! Yelled Zach while running full speed in the direction the bird flew. Greg gave chase yelling, "Zach, buddy, it's OK, we can….." Then he stopped himself from saying anything more. He just kept following Zach. The hawk still seemed to be having trouble gaining altitude and just as they neared the backyard pond the bird dropped Rum Rum. He fell through the air, legs kicking wildly, and hit the water making a splash. Greg was speechless. What could he or should he say. He remained silent.

Greg knelt down to Zach's level. He looked him in the eyes preparing to say something, anything, but still unsure of what. He hoped it would come out right. Then he noticed Zach's face did not have the pain and sadness that he expected it to show. "Daddy" Zach began; "The hawk gave Rum Rum a ride home. Now he has a really big bucket of water and lots of bugs he can eat and he will probably meet lots of frog friends too. I can come visit him anytime right?" "You got that right! You got that right!" Agreed Greg.

CHAPTER FIVE

Happy Birthday

The day before Greg had to leave for work, he got a call from his brother-in -law Wade, who told him Chuck McQuay, a neighbor in Foreston, had a donkey for sale.

Within the hour he had an "over the phone" gentleman's' handshake and an agreement to hold the donkey until Nessa birthday. This was going to be one BIG furry surprise. The family farm was growing.

The big day had finally arrived. All the relatives, neighbors and friends were invited to celebrate

Ally's and Nessa's birthday. Both Ally and Nessa had been looking forward to this day. Ally was pretty sure she would be getting her bike but Nessa had no idea the gift she would receive. Not a word had been spoken about a donkey since the night at the dinner table. She did not want to be told she wasn't getting a donkey so she didn't ask and she didn't ask for anything else either.

Grandma and Grandpa Hugg were the first to arrive, as usual. Grandpa could barely get out of the car before Zach was tackling him. It was a good trick to try to walk with the arms of a 4 yr. old wrapped around your legs and Grandpa loved every minute of it. He bent down and grabbed Zack's ankles, flipping him upside down and proceeded to twirl him like the spinning chair ride at the county fair. It was what Zack expected and so was the following "tongue lashing" Grandpa got from Grandma about how he was going to throw his back out or drop their precious Zach.

After her customary words of warning, Grandma headed for the house with her arms loaded with packages for the girls and a few jars of home canned dill pickles. Jen helped her with the door and hoped she would be the first to get a pickle before they were devoured by, soon to arrive, company.

A short distance from the house, the gravel road began a steady percolation of cars, making a sound as though someone continued to pour milk over Rice Crispies. Car after car began to arrive. The entire Hugg and Halstead families had been invited including aunts, uncles and cousins. It wasn't every day you could see a 7yr old get a surprise Donkey for her birthday.

Steph's brother Russ arrived with his wife and kids and right behind them were her other two brothers Wade and Brad.

Being a girl, with 3 younger brothers, she had learned to be the mothering type. She was protective, nurturing, tenacious (some would say stubborn), and had a heart that's flow was endless. Her brother Brad was 2nd oldest. He wasn't like the other kids. He was special in many ways. One time at around the age of 3 years. old he had completely disassembled the vacuum cleaner. Grandma Hugg was amazed by his interest to see how things came apart, even though it caused a bit more work in her day. This time she decided to ask Grandpa to put it back together, when he got home from work, but when she re-entered the room a bit later it had already been reassembled. Brad was smarter than most, he just followed a different path.

Steph's brothers taught her to be self-sufficient and fearless. She taught them to embrace and accept love in all forms. She was happy they were there for this special day.

The wagon train of cars had completed their destination and all guests were present and accounted for. The picnic tables were spattered with hot dishes, macaroni salad, potato salad, coleslaw, tater tot casserole, homemade potato sausage, 7-layer dip, rice cream, layered Jell-O, dump cake, rhubarb pie and fresh corn on the cob. There was sure to be a napping contest amongst the uncles in the afternoon.

Greg rang the triangle with the skill of a symphony conductor, "one two three, one two three," and the kids came running from the barn, pasture, and pond like rats in a flood. This wasn't their first beckon to eat at the Hallstead's.

The tables were lined with hungry folk and the flurry of food danced its way from plate to plate, table to table. A polka dance of passing, spooning, poking and plopping, slicing, forking and tossing, in perfect rhythm, ended in a slow quiet hum of chewing, smacking, and gulping. As tummies filled the tables began to empty as the Uncles took their place in the napping contest and cousins retreated to their tree climbing, pasture running, and pond rock skipping.

Grandma Hugg began clearing the table and like goslings following the mother goose, each Aunt follow suit. With the gaggle of team work the clean-up was done and the story telling ensued.

Nessa was having enough fun with her cousins and sisters, taking turns on the tire swing, to forget about the donkey she wouldn't get. The tire swing was the first of the kid's adornment to the property. Greg had located a perfect northern pin oak. It was close to the house; in direct view from the kitchen sink. It stood over 30 ft. tall with perfectly level outstretching branches that were waiting to be hung with bracelets of tire swings and climbing ropes.

Taking turns consisted of one cousin holding the tire, while the other climbed into the tire to get in perfect position; feet dangling out, butt tucked down into the open space and hands wrapped over top holding tight onto the rope. Steph had made it more comfortable, by placing an old pillow into the tire, so the kids back wouldn't rub on the rim. Next it was the wind up. It worked best with two working together, to spin the tire, until it was tightly fighting against them. Then they would give a push, back away and watch the rider holding on for dear life. The ride didn't seem to last long if you were watching but when it was your turn, somehow it was wound tighter than the last. No doubt, this phenomenon was the centrifugal force that made you feel as though the tree had joined in on trying to shake you free, to unleash your hands from the rope and pull the recent lunch from your tummy.

"Nessa it's your turn", said Jennifer. "That's OK, I'll just spin" said Nessa with her head down. "What's wrong?" asked Ally. "Nothing" she said as she started looking around the yard as if trying to locate someone specific. She had begun to think about the donkey she wanted. "Where's Dad"? Asked Nessa. Ally and Jennifer looked at each other. If Dad wasn't around, then it must be nearing time for the surprise of the year. "Oh he is probably going to go get my bike from where ever they have it hidden" stated Ally. "Come on Nessa, get on the tire swing. It's your turn. Dad and Mom will call for us when it's time to open presents" Pleaded Jennifer.

Nessa grabbed hold of the knot above the tire and swung one leg through the tire and then the next. She wriggled her tushy down into the pillow lined tire until appropriately snug and said" I'm ready". Jennifer and Ally took turns slapping the tire until it took both hands to push it. Tighter and tighter, taller and further up the rope the tire raised. It was time to let go.

As Ally backed away, the tire began its' unraveling and before Jennifer could get out of the way it struck her in the back sending her to the ground. This caused the tire to swing and spin wildly. Nessa's hands were holding on so tight that her tiny fingers were turning white. The force pulled her head back and then her bent arms began to stretch out as she tried to pull herself back up to the knot but the force was too strong and suddenly there was a bounce and her grip failed.

Nessa flew out of the tire swing like the chew from Uncle Lester's mouth. Just as Jennifer was on all fours to get up, Nessa landed square onto Jennifer's rear end landing them both face down. They both lay there silent. Ally was holding back the biggest laugh she had ever held while waiting for them to move.

Just then, both Nessa and Jennifer began laughing out of control while Ally and the other cousins joined in. From a distance it sounded like South African Hyenas enjoying an evening meal. The ring of the triangle sounded just in time to stop a belly laugh from becoming a belly ache. "Come on everyone; time for presents" hollered Steph.

Everyone was gathering around the biggest two picnic tables that were loaded with a bounty of gifts and cake. Nessa realized she had forgotten her disappointment that she would not be getting a donkey. She was having fun. Living on the farm was the best gift she could have been given and so she spent the next ½ hour, taking turns with Ally, opening the gifts that their friends and family had brought them. She was so enthralled she didn't notice that Dad was not there nor did she see him return.

Behind her she heard a familiar voice say "Two more presents to go" She turned and Dad was holding a beautiful shinny pink bike. Just what Ally had asked for. Ally ran over and gave both her Dad and her Mom a big hug. "I love it "she exclaimed. She swung her leg over the seat to check the feel. Her smile was so big she nearly lost her eyes in the squint it caused. "OK Nessa, your gift is over by the tire swing." Dad said.

Nessa wondered how it could be near the swing when they had just been there. Maybe it was a very small gift. But why then, by the tree? Was it a new tire? Maybe a real swing set like "town kids" have. But that didn't make any sense either. Maybe it was a blow-up pool so it would be shaded by the tree. Yea! Then we could swing from the tire and plop into the pool" she thought.

"Come on Nessa" Dad said, tugging her daydreaming body by her arm. Everyone followed close and as she neared the big oak tree she saw Grandpa Hugg come from behind the lilac bush holding a rope. Just as she was wondering, "what's he going to do with a rope", she realized it was not a rope but reins and reins connect to a bridle and if there is a bridle…She had learned all this from Great Grandpa Snow. Their farm was just up the road from Grandpa and Grandma Hugg's house. Great Grandpa Snow was Grandma Hugg's Papa. He had all kinds of animals and Nessa's favorite was the Shetland pony; a perfect size for her. Her last visit there, Grandpa let her walk the pony and she got to hold the reins. So if Grandpa Hugg was holding reins then that meant………

Just then, the nose of the cutest donkey in the world pushed past the lilacs. The donkey gave a sniff, as it continued toward Nessa. She was frozen. She couldn't move her legs. She began to believe she was dreaming. Maybe she had hit her head when thrown from the tire swing and was still out. Grandpa Hugg kneeled before her, looked into her clear blue eyes, and handed her the reins. Still she did not move.

She suddenly felt her dad put his hand on her shoulder and the spell was broken. She reached out her hand to touch the donkey's snowy white muzzle and he met her half way, as he butted up to meet her hand. She petted his coco brown head and then his fluffy velvet ears. His white chest seemed to grow like a puffer fish with every touch Nessa gave him. The donkey's long eyelashes flickered as if he was embarrassed, like a school boy with a crush. Then he nudged her arm wanting more! She reached out with both arms wide and hugged her new best friend.

The surprise was a success and the talk of everyone's conversation over the next few weeks. The gift of a donkey, to a tiny 7yr old, blonde haired, blue eyed girl, even made the Mille Lacs County Times social column.

CHAPTER SIX

Say His Name

Even without an alarm or a rooster to wake her, it would be a good bet that Nessa would be first to place her feet upon the hardwood floors of the old farmhouse. She was always an early riser and her new motivation to get dressed and outside was just a football field away in the pasture.

The sun had barely peeked its way through the row of pines that lined the long drive. The rays of sun created a spray of misty orange light directly onto the open pasture. The show was about to begin.

Nessa opened her eyes abruptly and "wide eyed". She had been dreaming that she had finally gotten the donkey she had prayed for. She had been rubbing his ears and scratching his head. He had been tickling her under her arm by moving his lips up and down. She was giggling and in the dream she said "Francis that tickles" as he nudged her with his nose she awoke. "His name is Francis. Yes, Francis. That's his name." She thought. Then it hit her. What if this had been but a dream?

She popped out of bed, slipped on her boots, grabbed her jacket and ran down stairs. She flew out the back door toward the pasture. As she was running she scanned from left to right looking for the black and brown fur she longed to hug. As she neared the sun lit stage of the pasture, her heart began to beat faster. Where was he? Had it really only been a dream?

She stopped short of the gate and let out the deep breath she had been holding for the last 50 feet. Where was he? She looked back at the house. The pines swayed slightly in the morning breeze causing the sunlight to twinkle into her eyes.

When she turned her attention back to the pasture it took a moment for her eyes to adjust. A shadow in the distance began to come into focus. She blinked her blue eyes feverishly, straining for adjustment and then squeezed them tight. Nessa slowly opened her eyes and there he was. His slow deliberate gate directly in her path.

Nessa was now standing on the bottom rale of the fence reaching her arms out to her dream come true. Five feet from her reached-out hand the donkey stopped. He put his big white nose in the air and belted out "Hee Haw" "Hee Haw" and proceeded to take a bow. This would be the first of many performances on the "Halstead farms pasture stage" and Francis would not be the only performer!

Steph stood at the kitchen window as the smell of fresh brewed coffee began to perfume the air. Her heart so full she could hardly hold back the tears as she watched her little girl fall in love. She could see that Nessa was talking to her donkey; even using her hands when she spoke. Little did she know; Nessa was singing him a song she made up just for him. Nessa sang (to the tune of Twinkle Twinkle Little Star)

Francis, Francis come and play.
Let's have lots of fun today,
We can walk or I can ride.
Carrots fuel your snail's-pace stride.
Francis, Francis you're my friend.
I'll be with you till the end.

Steph remembered her first pet. Her folks had begun raising pigs. One sow was close to farrowing (delivering her piglets) and she remembered her mom saying that it was likely that some of the baby pigs may not survive. She told her that sometimes they don't even take a breath and some are smaller and may have to work so hard to fight the bigger ones to eat, that they too do not make it.

So when the 11 piglets were born, one in fact did not take a breath. And sure enough there was a piglet that was much smaller than the others.

The bigger piglets pushed past the little one, never giving it a chance to get milk. She recalled asking her Mom if they could give it a bowl of milk. Her Mom explained that they aren't able to drink like that yet.

The only hope for this little one would be to hand feed it with a bottle. "Steph" Her Mom said, "it will be a lot of work, especially the first day and I will help and then it will be every 3-4 hours to feed it and it still may not survive, but if you want to try, you could hand fed the runt." Steph took on the challenge.

She named the piglet Pinky because it was pure pink. Before and after school she was feeding Pinky every 3-4 hours.

It wasn't long before Pinky was drinking from a bowl and catching up with her brothers and sisters. Yet to Pinky, Steph was Mom. Anytime Steph was in the yard, Pinky was her shadow.

Now it was Nessa's turn, with Francis, to know the feeling of caring for another with unconditional love in return.

Zach was the next of the kids to get out of bed. He came into the kitchen holding onto his Superman blankie and asking Steph "Where's Nessa?" "She is outside with her donkey" she replied. Before she could turn around from flipping pancakes, he had dropped his blankie and run out the door. "don't go into the pasture" she hollered after him.

She moved to the window to see Zach running in Nessa's direction. He jumped onto the first rung of the fence, stretching to get closer to the donkey. It appeared Nessa was introducing Zach to the donkey. After a quick pat on its nose Zach came running back into the house.

Steph stepped away from the window just in time to flip the almost overdone pancake. Zach flew in the house, like the superman he had left on the floor. I met him! I met him! I know his name.

"Really? How exciting! What is his name Zach?" Asked Steph. "It's Kansas" said Zach. "Kansas? Well that's an interesting name for a donkey" said Steph.

"Kansas?" Asked Jennifer as she walked into the kitchen. "We are going to Kansas?" Jen inquired.

"No. We're not going to Kansas. Kansas is the name Zach tells me that Nessa has named her donkey." Said Steph.

Just then Nessa came in the door and asked; is breakfast ready?

"Pancakes are done and sausage is close. So Kansas huh?" asked Steph.

"What?" said Nessa. "Your donkeys' name. Zach told us" said Steph. "Mom, my donkeys name is Francis" said Nessa. Jen and Steph began to laugh.

It wasn't the first time Zach made a funny translation.

CHAPTER SEVEN

Back to School

It seemed like only weeks had gone by since the move to the country home but the summer had passed like the few minutes you get from one of those mechanical pony rides in front of the grocery store. School would begin in only a week and Steph still had a few things on the list to buy. And then there was the task of preparing three little girls for their first long bus ride. Although it would probably be easier than preparing Dad.

When they had talked about it a few weeks prior, he had wondered if they would be safe; would they sit in their seats? Would they get scared or get off the bus at the wrong house? Steph had attempted to calm his fears. "Greg, she said, I rode the bus from the time I was 5 years. old until you started picking me up in my junior year. They will be fine. Those three girls are made from our tough cloth and together they can stand up to anyone and anything!" The pep talked helped and Greg focused instead on his upcoming trip out of town for work.

The specialty concrete flooring business would, this time, take him away for 3 weeks. One time he was sent to Thailand for nearly two months and he vowed he would never be gone that long again. Luckily Steph could do and fix just about anything and if something happened while he was gone, her Mom and Dad were only 4 miles down the road from the new house.

Greg left early the next morning, while the kids were still hugging their pillows. He did not want to wake them, having only one more week of sleeping in late before school would begin.

Steph got her back-to-school list completed and suddenly the first day of school had come and gone. It went far easier than she had expected. The girls thought the adventure of a bus ride was magical. It seems that Grandpa Hugg had told them some amazing stories of the places buses could take them.

He had told them that buses were a place for imagination. If they concentrated on the sounds that the bus makes, while going down the road, it could take them anywhere. Grandpa Hugg said "The engine makes a special sound and if you listen closely, really closely, with your eyes closed, you will hear it. The clank and the cling and the shimmy and the chatter and soon you will hear it. You will feel it. You are on the train; the train that will take you far into the jungle.

There will be gigantic trees that have leaves the size of an elephant's ear. If you push your ear to the window, you can hear the branches brushing the sides of the train, slapping it Hello "welcome to the Jungle".

As the train slows you may hear the squeaks of the gymnastics from the Monkeys swinging from limb to limb, while big beaked birds with colorful wings of purple and blue, swoop down to pluck berries from the bushes.

Now take a deep breath Grandpa said, a really deep breath in you will smell the sweetness of the berries. If you hear a rumbling sound like a thunderstorm making its way home, you will probably be nearing the waterfalls. They sore so high in the sky that the clouds get blown into them and disappear in the mist."

He told them he would share of the other places the bus could take them, after the first week of school. Well his strategy worked. The girls got on the bus without tears or fears.

So the girls made it off that morning and within fifteen minutes of the school bus picking them up, Zach asked if the girls would be home soon. He seemed concerned.

It took a few questions for Steph to realize why and then convinced Zach that they would come back from the Jungle that Grandpa had told them about. He then settled into digging up and planting his imaginary farm with his new matchbox tractor.

Steph took the opportunity to go upstairs and make the beds, gather laundry and open the windows. She wrote out a few checks to pay some bills, sent a thank you note to her Mom and Dad for their help moving and then gathered up Zach to go into town. She stopped at the creamery for milk and butter then got a small load of groceries. She treated Zach to a hot dog and Ice cream at Dairy Queen.

After Zach helped her unload the groceries, he was ready for his afternoon nap. While he napped, she worked on canning the jars of pickles and beets from her garden as her mother had taught her. Zach was still asleep when the last jars were done, so she sat on the couch, put her feet up and closed her eyes.

She was dreaming that she and Greg were on a tropical island. They were sitting near the ocean and monkeys were coming up to them, eating fruit from their hands, when one of the monkeys screeched in anger, as another got the mango before him. It woke her and she realized she could hear the sound of the school bus brakes as it slowed at the end of the road; 2:20 and right on time. She shook the sleepiness off and grabbed the plate of snacks she had ready and waiting. This was not the only thing waiting for them. Zach had come out of his room and now had his nose pressed so hard against the window, watching for the bus, that it was red when he eventually pulled it away.

He ran for the door and was met by Nessa who nearly ran him over as she bolted inside. "Mom! Mom! I won! I won! I traded and got an even better prize", exclaimed Nessa. "You traded what? Won what?" asked her Mother as she finished wiping dry the last of the jars she was preparing for canning.

Nessa went on to share that her class had a "special back to school" reading fun day. Each child was asked to read a paragraph from a book and then after doing so, had the opportunity to choose a mystery prize from the covered box. "My prize was a toy truck, but I didn't really want it. So when I was on the bus I traded with Ian Miskowic." Said Nessa

Ian Miskowic is on your bus? Asked Steph. His grandparents own Miskowic Farms, where we get our meat. I forgot their kids live out this way. "Yea Mom, do you want to see what I got?" asked Nessa. Steph placed the jar, she had been holding, onto the counter and went closer. Nessa lifted her metal "My Little Pony" lunch box carefully against her chest.

The box seemed to be shifting in her tiny hands as if there were an invisible force trying to take it from her. While holding tightly to the bottom, Nessa slowly opened the metal clasp.

There, peering up from the snug fitted metal box, sat a little yellow chick. Nessa looked up at her Mom with her sparkling blue eyes, as big as gem doughnuts, hoping for approval. "well isn't it the cutest little chick I've ever seen." her Mother said, Nessa's pensive smile grew. "Does this mean I can keep it?" asked Nessa. "Yes Nessa, you can keep the chick" replied Steph. "I am going to name her name her "Chick"." Nessa told her Mom with Excitement.

Steph worked with Nessa on the "ins and outs" of "Chick care" It would require constant care and monitoring. They talked about keeping Chick in the garage. At first Nessa wanted to keep her in the bedroom in a box near her bed. Steph had to explain that chicks love to scratch and so all her bedding, food and poop may end up on the floor or her toys and as they get bigger the more the mess.

They found a great apple box and set it up in the Garage. "Baby chicks need to be kept pretty hot. About 90 degrees, going down by 5 degrees, per week, until they're ready to transition to outside. Steph explained.

So they bought a 250-watt infrared heat lamp at the hardware store and placed it at the edge so it heated the box to just the right temperature. They lined the bed with pine shavings and got a water dispenser, feeder and feed from Foreston Farms Co-Op Creamery. Nessa had no idea one tiny chick could need so much.

The first few weeks Nessa would check on Chick every morning before breakfast and throughout the day and before going to bed. She made sure she had water, food and her bed was clean. As the time past the need to check on Chick decreased but not Nessa's need to take care of her.

It wasn't until Chick was about 3 months old that Uncle Aldie was over for a visit that he informed Nessa she had a roster not a hen. He showed Nessa the hackle and saddle feathers on Chick and pointed out how long and skinny they were." This is a sign of a Boy chicken called a Roster" he told her. "You will know for sure when he begins to crow when he gets a little older." He said.

It wasn't long after that "Chicks" demeanor began to change. He liked to chase the kids; especially when they were walking home from the pond. As he grew, he could run faster and eventually could keep up with the kids.

His favorite attack was to wait behind the garage and as the kids rounded the corner he would give chase and with a running jump, plant both feet into the back of the victim's legs. It's been said if you and a friend are hiking and come upon a bear, you need not outrun the bear, only the other hiker.

And so it was with Chick. The moment they saw him the race was on. Eventually he was renamed "Petey the Claw" And yes he did crow.

CHAPTER EIGHT

Wake up Call

As with most Saturdays, the day began with a slower start. No alarms to break the silence of the quiet country air. Sure, Petey the claw gave his timely 5:30 am muffled "cock-a-doodle-do". But it was mild now compared to the first time he belted out his obnoxious morning alarm.

The first day Petey found his voice Greg had imagined a fox had him cornered in the coop. Even though he was an ankle chasing crazy bird he was part of the family, so Greg had to get up and save him from sure death. He grabbed his pants from the laundry basket and pulled them on while trying to get through the bedroom door but they were still covering his feet. The denim slipped on the freshly waxed floors and sent one leg out into the hall while the other remained inside. "Splits" was not on his list of perfected gymnastic moves. Fortunately, the crotch of his Levis, now at the level of his thigh, held firm keeping him for certain injury. He got back on his feet and jumped up and down trying to raise his pants to the proper level.

Meanwhile Steph was busy shoving the comforter in her mouth to muffle the laughter that was trying to escape. He pulled himself together, grabbed his shotgun and flashlight, then headed down the hall to the rescue. He pensively made his way over to the coop and switched on his flashlight hoping to catch the predator in the act. Petey was still screeching his "off tune" cock-a-doodle-do when the light hit him. There he was, perched atop the feeder. His beak in the air, neck stretched, wings tight at his side, nearly standing on his tip toes. No predator in sight just Petey giving the morning air his concert debut. He had found his voice and was proud.

After about a week of this obnoxious morning hullabaloo, Greg had had enough. He was just about ready to treat Petey with a trip to the local 4-H, when Steph drove up the driveway. She had known Greg's frustration was growing so she had been asking all the farmers, during her grocery run, if they had any suggestions as to how to quiet a rooster.

Ralph Jones, from the Foreston Co-op, said his Grandad used to put their noisy rooster in a small cage at dusk, to prevent it from standing tall enough to get a good crow started in the morning. So after picking up groceries, Steph hit the Co-op again, to buy a small cage and made her way home.

She was just pulling the cage out of the trunk when Greg came outside. "Hi honey, I am on my way to the Foreston Forgers 4-H club to donate Petey" Said Greg. He then noticed that Steph was holding a small cage. "Oh Great" he said, "Thanks I can use this to carry Petey from the coop." "No" said Steph. "It's not to take him, it's to help him not crow or crow softer. "How does that work" asked Greg. Steph shared what Farmer Jones told her about how if the cage is smaller than Petey is, when he stands stretched tall, he can't crow as loud.

Greg was skeptical, yet he knew it was worth a try, to save some small hearts from hurting. They would have been sure to miss the occasional ankle attack. The first night in the cage proved the theory true.

While Petey began his early morning attempt to sing the usual rendition of revelry, it did not have the same level of screech or howl. It went from an unbearable cry for help to a distant sound of tires stopping abruptly on pavement. The family learned to sleep through the modified daily alarm.

So with the rise of the sun the week-end began. The usual order of descend down the stairs began with Nessa, Zach following close behind. Jen and Ally were later sleepers. Jen and Ally had plans for play dates with friends from school and Zach was going fishing with Grandpa Hugg. Greg left the night before to join some friends up north for a week-end motorcycle ride. The day would be just Steph and Nessa.

The kitchen came alive as Steph fried the maple bacon that came from the Miskowic Family Farms in Princeton. Nothing better than local farms raised pork and beef. The smell floated up the stairs as if being delivered by a lost balloon, bouncing off the wall, flowing down the hall, through the open bedroom door and right under Jennifer's nose. The snake charming smell of bacon rose her from the bed down the stairs, before she could even fully wipe the sleepy from her eyes.

Nessa came in from outside where she had been saying good morning to Francis. Chores were done before the girls left for the day and Steph was caught up on her housework. So it was a quiet day on the farm for Nessa and her mother. She decided to take this rare opportunity to work on reupholstering a chair she had gotten at a local estate sale, while Nessa would draw pictures. She gathered all her tools, situated the chair in the garage and began the task of de-constructing. This was the easy part. She was good at demo. She and Greg did all the demo on the remodeled bathrooms and kitchen. It goes fast and you see progress.

It had been such a long time that she had worked on a fun project, without interruption that she was shocked when she realized she had been wrestling with the chair for nearly two hours.

With a bit of guilt, not fear, she sprinted into the house to check in on Nessa. "Hey Nessa" she called out, as she entered the house. "How's it going" she asked. She got to the top of the stairs and all was quiet. She poked her head around the door jamb into Nessa and Ally's room. She was not there. Her papers were spread out on the floor but no Nessa. A tinge of worry began to build. She dropped the stairs two at a time calling out "Nessa where are you?" a brief pause for reply and out the door she went. Nessa! Nessa! Where are you?" No answer. She scanned the yard. First the pasture. She was sure to be with Francis but at first glance Francis was missing too. But then she saw him at the peak of the grassy knoll laying on his side, basking in the sun. No Nessa.

True panic began to set in. She was a good swimmer but any body of water had its dangers and the pond was full of vegetation. She knew not to go there without an adult but where else could she be? Nessa where are you!" She hollered again.

Just before she walked to the garage, to hop on the quad, she looked one more time in Francis direction. Just then the wind kicked up beyond the pines and shot a gust of wind past her in the direction of the Francis. Steph followed it with her eyes as it seemed to target the knoll like a lit fuse. It hit Francis and sent, what appeared to be a puff of yellow smoke from his belly. Again this yellow twirl rose from the sleeping belly of Nessa best friend.

Steph ran to the pasture. She scaled the split rail fence and with her right leg dangling over the top rung and her left foot planted on the other side of the bottom rung she stopped.

Perched on the fence like a Red Tailed Hawk focusing in on its prey, she squinted her eyes to telescope her vision on Francis. Now she could see just beyond the silhouette of Francis reclining form. Hidden in the protective curve of his belly, lay a golden haired angel, asleep on the "pillow" of a donkey.

CHAPTER NINE

Friendship

Over the next few years, their bond would create a love few would ever experience. If Nessa had a reading assignment, she read to him. They went on walks together. Nessa rarely used reins, as Francis followed her every move. He would have followed her into the house, if it weren't for the broom Steph had determined worked to stop his persistent request for entry.

She learned to ride and Francis seemed proud when she rode with him. He was so gentle. It was as though he was balancing a fragile plate atop his back. Each hoof was placed slowly to the ground with precision. One hoof, then the next. At first his deliberate gait created a swaying saunter where Nessa resembled an African princess atop a royal elephant.

Over time Francis felt Nessa's confidence and slowly relaxed his walk and would even run at her insistence.

The weather of fall brought perfect riding conditions for Francis and Nessa. He started getting his winter coat and she could bundle up, making the ride more comfortable for both of them. Nessa asked her mom if she could make a picnic lunch, so she and Francis could go to the pond and have an adventure, as she had done a few times.

Greg and Steph had built a rustic, small 175 square foot cabin directly in front of the pond. While only a few football fields away, the family was able to enjoy afternoons of fishing, canoe riding, bar-b-ques and occasional sleep-overs without leaving the property.

So Steph said yes and supervised Nessa preparing her meal. Nessa made her own peanut butter and jelly sandwich, put a few cookies in a bag and poured some juice in a jar. Steph threw in a sandwich bag of cut apple. "Don't forget to grab some carrots out of the barn for Francis" Said Steph. "OK Mom I will and I won't forget the "walkie talkie"! Replied Nessa.

The radios had proven to be a great investment for the farm. Greg had picked up the first pair at an auction with no intention but for the kids to play with them around the house. Then after the sixth or seventh trip from the barn to the house for an item or two, that he had forgotten, he decided that a walkie talkie in the Barn and garage and the house, would save him a few steps. He could signal the house and ask for one of the kids to make a delivery. The used pair didn't have great reception, so talk was scratchy, buy they worked. Then they realized the newer models had better range and so they bought three sets. One designated for the Garage and one for the barn. The third would be rover for the property. If any of the kids went for a quad ride, long walk out to the pond, they would take a walkie talkie.

It had become evident that Zach was interested in technology and talk so he was the director of communications. He taught the girls to wait a moment before they began to talk while pushing the talk button and to be sure to set the same frequency as the other handset. He did his research on two-way radio terms and etiquette. "Breaker 1-9" meant that you want to start a transmission or a conversation. "10-4" was Okay and "Big 10-4" meant Yes. "Roger That" let the other person know that you Understood and "Over and Out" signaled you were done talking. There were terms for some of the same meanings and all the kids had fun drilling each other on how many they could get right.

"*Negatory*" No, "*Affirmative*" Yes,
"*Do you copy?*" Can you hear me?

"*Copy that*" I heard you."

"*What's your handle?*" What's your nickname?
"*Got your ears on?*" Are you on air

"*What's your 20?*" Where are you?

So with the education of an enthusiastic communications director the radios became a routine tool at the Halstead farm.

"I'm glad you remembered the radio Nessa. You are becoming so responsible." Said Steph

"Thanks Mom. I didn't even need you to reminded me to take them!" Said Nessa as she lifted her picnic backpack and grabbed the walkie talkie from the bowl on the hall tree. She gave the battery test button a test push" and the green light lit. She shoved the radio into her pack and reached for the door.

"Hold on sweetie, I need my kiss and here is a sheet to put down for your picnic." Insisted Steph "Nessa swiftly dropped her hand from the door and spun around to give her Mom a hug and a kiss, grabbed the sheet, then out the door she went.

As she skipped to the barn to grab a load of carrots, she hollered "Francis wanna go for a ride?" Immediately Francis began to bray "Hee Haw! Hee Haw!" while he reared with excitement. Nessa dropped her backpack, freeing both hands to pull open the barn door. She was pretty good at it by now.

Just inside, from the tack wall, she grabbed the bridle and threw it over her shoulder. On the floor was the bucket of carrots. Nessa popped the lid, pulled 5 carrots and closed the lid. She dropped the carrots into the backpack and closed the barn door.

Francis began his singing again. Well, he thought he was singing, but to most folks it was a Howl and a squeal. The first week they had him, two different neighbors stopped, while driving past the house, to see if everything was OK, thinking one of the kids was terribly injured. Neither of them got to the front door before they realized it was Francis.

Nessa picked up the backpack and made her way over to the pasture, where Francis was bowing and rearing and dancing with excitement. She set the backpack on the ground and let the bridle fall from her shoulder and caught it in her hand. She stood on the first rung of the fence and leaned against the top rung.

"Come here Francis, put your head down" she said. The commands were soft but the response strong. He followed her commands like a well-trained dog competing at Westminster Kennel Club. Nessa placed the bit into his mouth, as she put the crown of the bridle over his ears and adjusted the brow band. She took hold of the reins and lay them over Francis neck. "Come here Francis" coaxed Nessa, as she slapped the top rail of the fence.

While Francis sidestepped over and put his back parallel to the enclosure that kept him in the pasture Nessa put on her back pack then climbed back on the fence. Nessa bent her left knee and place it on the top rail and push herself into a standing position while holding onto to Francis neck. She then swung her right leg over Francis back. Time for an adventure.

Francis and Nessa made a slow journey across the pasture to the west edge, where the Maple trees lined the grass. This was their favorite place to begin the ride.

This time of year the maple trees were flourished with large leaves of amber, red and yellow, the size of baseball mitts. The trees could not help but be generous and shared their leaves with Nessa. She picked them to use on her adventures. They served as place mats, fans, skirts and bowls for picking wild strawberries. Francis even let Nessa make him a hat one sunny day.

Nessa guided Francis between two of the tallest Maples. As she passed them, she imagined they bowed to her, as would the guards at the entrance of the castle. "Princess Nessa, of the forest, arriving on her royal donkey" they announced.

As they entered the thickness of the trees, the temperature cooled and brought the fragrance of the wilderness floor; moist grass, layered leaves, and sweet fern. Francis and Nessa inhaled the natural incense as they journeyed farther into the depths of the royal forest.

Grey squirrels began to race to the tips of the tree branches to get a glimpse of the princess. The whistle and jeers of the blue jays, the melodic flute of the oriole and the warbles and trills of the sparrow made music on their approach. She was back and they couldn't wait for the treat she would share.

CHAPTER TEN

Adventure

The royal forest soon opened up into a meadow, where the sun brought the warmth of a fresh blanket just pulled from the dryer. The edge of the forest provided shade but the sun's rays were needed this time of year. Here is where she would share lunch with her royal court. Nessa slipped down from Francis's back to the grassy carpet of the meadow below. She put her thumbs under the straps of the back pack and let it fall behind her. Next she pulled out the sheet and let the breeze catch it like a flag and lowered it to the grass.

Out came the apples, sandwich, carrots and juice. Francis inched his way over to the sheet like Grandpa pushing his walker. One short step and pause, next step and pause. "you are being so patient" said Nessa. She laid out the spread and took half her sandwich from the bag. She could hear the birds raise their pitch in anticipation. Nessa took a bite of the sandwich and grabbed a carrot. She reached it up to Francis. He met her half way and with gentle hesitation he opened his mouth. His upper lip rolled back showing his big teeth as she slipped the carrot between his jaws and he gave a precise crunch. Then again, for the remainder of the carrot.

Nessa took an apple piece and broke it in half then tossed one half into the meadow and the other a few feet away from the first. It wasn't long before the birds took turn snacking on the feast that lay before them. As they ate their apple Francis devoured another carrot.

Nessa unfolded the big leaves she had collected and lay them out on the sheet. One would be for the Princess jewels, another for her comb and brush and the other for the special perfume. She got up from the sheet and walked over to a pine tree, a few yards away. Perfect she thought, as she collected a pine cone. This would be her brush. Then she snapped a low branch of pine needles. This would be her comb. She scanned the ground for diamonds and gold to fill her jewelry box. A beautiful rock with gold glitter appeared from under the leaves as she kicked the ground. She scooped it up and searched for more. She was so focused on collecting jewelry from the ground, she hadn't noticed the sky changing its colors from blue and clear to grey and cloudy. Just as she bent down, to examine another find, she heard the sky give warning with a slow rumble. She looked up and saw the sky becoming angry.

"Francis, we gotta get home. Sounds like rain!' She said aloud. Quickly Nessa gathered her sheet and shoved it into the backpack. She pulled on Francis's reins, guiding him close to a tree and used a branch to pull herself up onto Francis's back. Let go home Francis.

Just then a loud clap of thunder shot out of the sky and startled Francis. He began to run. "It's OK" yelled Nessa, as she bounced back and forth, holding her knees tight to Francis's belly to keep from sliding off. "Whoa! Slow down she pleaded" She held on to his reins, as he navigate back and forth between the trees like receiver with a football. His pace persisted and she could see he was headed straight toward a tree with a long reaching branch. "Who Francis, slow down" she screamed again, but it was too late. She quickly ducked down, flat against Francis's back like a jockey. She felt herself being lifted off of Francis back. She expected to hit the ground anytime, but that didn't happen.

The tree, that had bowed to her majesty on the way in, had reached out and taken her captive. There she hung by her back pack, 6 feet off the ground.

Francis had stopped and turned around as soon as he felt his back become lighter. He stood there staring up at her. Nessa kicked her legs as she swayed. The branch had found the space between the backpack and Nessa's back. The weight of her body pulled the straps at her shoulders, keeping her arms away from her body. She couldn't reach the straps to set herself free.

Another rumble began. The sky was hungry and would soon crack another warning, that rain was coming. "OK Francis you have to help me" she said. "Come here. Get closer" she urged, as she kicked her feet. Francis took a step in her direction and paused, looked up at her and stopped. "What are you waiting for Francis?" she said. He took another step closer. He was two feet from her when the sky took another crack of the whip. Francis shuddered his feet moving as though he was standing on hot coals, but he didn't run. He quickly got under Nessa and she bent her knees then balance her feet on his back. He stood taller and she pushed off his back to attempt to wiggle loose from her captor. She jumped, jumped, jumped and the 4th time she slipped out of the backpack landing in splits over Francis back. Nessa grabbed his reins. "Let's go home Francis "she said.

Francis walked briskly out of the woods into the pasture and then over to the fence where their journey had begun. Nessa got off Francis back and as she stood on the fence, she bent down and gave Francis a huge hug. "Thank you for saving me, my knight in shining armor!!

As Nessa walked into the house Steph said "Oh! I'm so glad you came home early. It looks like we may have rain. How was your ride? And hey, where is your back pack?" "Mom, I could use a nap. Can I fill you in after I wake up? A nap for Nessa? Thought her Mom. That was unusual. Steph nodded her head and said "sure" She couldn't wait to hear what had her so pooped.

CHAPTER ELEVEN

Sharing

Nessa sat anxiously on the back porch, waiting for her best friend Stacee to come over for the day. She was so much fun to spend the day with. They both loved animals, adventures, and even some of the girl stuff, like dress up and playing with dolls, so they never were bored

Stacee came riding up the driveway wearing her pink cowboy boots. She was on her pink fendered bike complete with a white basket, trumpet horn and sparkled handle-bar fringe, that slapped in the air as she peddled at top speed. It was a Girley bike but the girl on it was anything but.

Nessa recalled the first time she met Stacee. They were at a 4-H competition at the county fair. Nessa had Petey the Claw entered in the Rooster Crowing contest and Stacee had an entry too. Petey's cage was right next to Stacee's entry in the building that shared space with chickens, ducks, turkeys, goats and sheep.

That day the Minnesota humidity was high so the air was thick with the smells of sweet hay, manure and an occasional whiff of cinnamon rolls, that were baking just outside the west entrance. To the east you could hear the squeals of the riders on the Zipper and Wipeout and the distant music from the Round up. Nessa was excited to be there not only to see all the animals and go on a few rides but mostly because she and her family were going to see the Dixie Chicks concert that night.

Deep in thought, about how exciting her first concert would be, she opened the door to Petey's cage and just then Stacee walked up next to her. As Nessa looked up to say hi to Stacee, Petey scrambled through the door faster than Nessa could reached out after him and she slipped on the hay, falling to the ground.

Without pause, Stacee gave chase after Petey. She sprinted through the strolling visitors; dodging and weaving. Hearing the commotion, they stepped aside on her approach, pointing and laughing at the run-away rooster. As Petey past the goats Stacee saw the main door that opened to the fun zone. "If he got out there it would be over." She thought. She put her feet into high gear and focused on the evading escapee.

She was gaining on him, in hot pursuit, as if following a bank robber with a load of cash, when a woman pushing a stroller came across the aisle directly in front of her. Without hesitation, and no time to do so, she hurdled over the stroller with the ease of an Olympic track star and dove after Petey. Nessa had been following close behind and saw Stacee clear the stroller, landing her right foot and then flying forward directly on top of Petey. They both skid cross the floor past two turkey cages and a boy with an Ice Cream cone before they came to a stop.

"Are you OK"? said the woman in the stroller. "Need some help"? asked a man wearing overhauls and a green John Deer ball cap.

Nessa pushed past the concerned crowd and bend down to see if Petey survived being crushed by this strange girl. "I got him!" exclaimed Stacee as she rolled over onto her back, holding Petey in the air like a prize while keeping a firm grip around the fleeing felon. Nessa took Petey from her grip and held him out, to view him from all angles. Not a feather out of place!

By then, Stacee had gotten off the floor and was bushing straw off her pants. "Your welcome" said Stacee sarcastically to Nessa. "Huh?" said Nessa. "I saved your bird from sure death. He is a pretty fast rooster but no one can beat me in sprint." Stated Stacee beaming with pride. "Oh yea, um Thank you" said Nessa, a bit unsure of weather she was even grateful this stranger gave chase to her rooster. "That was pretty cool the way you flew over the stroller. "she continued as they walked back to the rooster cages. Stacee patted Nessa on the back and said "I've got money for ice cream if you wanna get one? And so began the long friendship that would be complete with the adventures the farm life could deliver.

Nessa ran up the road to meet Stacee. "My Mom said you can stay for dinner if you want to and she can give you a ride back home, if it is OK with your Mom" Said Nessa, jogging along-side of Stacee's bike, as she peddled the rest of the way up the drive "OK, I'll call my mom when we get inside. Said Stacee.

What do you want to do first?" asked Nessa. "Let's go see Francis"! Replied Stacee. "He's still out beyond the pasture. Let's wait till he gets closer to home. How about playing on the tire swing." Said Nessa. "OK "Stacee agreed as she hopped off her bike and lowered it to the ground. Then off they ran.

They took turns pushing each other as high as they could and winding the tire tight to produce the "dizzies" that came after letting go. The giggles that followed were as much fun to recover from. After about an hour, they headed inside the house, to ask for a snack.

Steph was at the kitchen table stitching on some seat covers, for the vintage yellow Corvette that Greg had surprised her with for their 10th anniversary. She had been watching the girls on and off, out the kitchen window. Knowing Nessa, she would be ready to refuel that "hummingbirds body of hers, so she had already prepared for a drink and snack break.

Nessa and Stacee came through the kitchen door at a pace of urgency. Steph knew the look of a "too long ignored" bladder and watched them head straight to the bathroom. The sound of the flush and running of the sink signaled their exit and out they popped like Eggos from a toaster. "Mom may we have a snack" said Nessa before realizing the mid-morning spread was already on the table. "Thanks Mr. Halstead" said Stacee, eyeing it just as Nessa did. On the table was a bowl of sliced cucumbers, cheese squares and homemade strawberry jam to slather atop the fresh bread that Greg had picked up from Weisbrod's bakery on his way home the night before. Neither Foreston or Milaca, the towns closest to the farm, had a bakery. So whenever Steph or Greg went through Princeton, they would stop at Weisbrod's to get fresh made loafs.

The girls sat down and plated up. Then began their individual eating rituals. Nessa started with a crunch of a cucumber, a nibble of cheese, followed by a lick off the mound of jam on a slice of the bread. When the jam was but a thin pink memory against the white soft jam holder, Nessa rolled the slice like a cigar, took a few imaginary puffs then devoured it! Stacee made her cucumber sandwich by placing a smashed cheese square between two cucumber slices. She also made an imaginary cigar however hers was rolled with all the jam inside.

Having eaten nearly all the food from the table, they were ready to move on. Nessa got the step stool and put it in front of the sink. Stacee handed her the dirty dishes and she rinsed them in the sink. "That's good enough girls" said Steph. "I have a surprise for you." She reached into her sewing box and pulled out two blueberry lollipops. "Take them with you." "Blueberry! My favorite. Thanks Mom." "Thanks Mrs. Halstead" said Nessa and Stacee "Let's go play in the barn" said Nessa. "Yea!" replied Stacee and out the door they went.

The barn was a great place for imagination. It was complete with strange tools, unfamiliar equipment and other items that were unrecognizable. Depending on the time of year, it had different smells too. Never bad, but musty like Grandmas basemen or wet leaves and sometimes sweet from the hay. The rafters above gave birds, squirrels and other moving creatures, an elevated highway across the barn. If you were below, when the highway was occupied, your head or back could be the recipient of a falling nut, flying hay or a wet, stinky bird poop. That was all part of the fun. To see if you could enter the barn and come out without screaming, running or at worst crying.

Nessa and Stacee stopped short of going inside the barn. It was here they would gather their courage. They strategized about how they could stay within the barn, even if one of them became scared. Nessa wasn't scared, if Francis was with her, but completely alone was another story. Stacee suggested that they hold hands. They both agreed that wouldn't work, if they wanted to climb the ladder to the hayloft. They finally agreed if one got scared enough to run, they would meet at the door and wait for the other.

Nessa pulled back the rolling door on the barn. Immediately barn swallows flew out past her directly in Stacee's path. She whipped her head back and ducked in time to miss a direct hit by their escape but fell backwards from the momentum. The girls looked at each other and the belly laughs began for the second time that day.

Nessa put out her hand and helped pull Stacee up from the ground. "Let's go inside" She said.

It was almost noon so there was no sunlight coming in from the sides so the barn remained fairly dark. They walked slowly, to allow time for their eyes to adjust to the darkness. Turning on the lights wasn't allowed in this adventure. Stacee walked over to the tack bench. Under the bench was the carrot bucket. She dragged it out from under the bench and positioned it just in front. Putting her hands on the bench to stabilizer herself she placed one foot on the bucket and then the other. She balanced herself in a squatting position looking like a hen sitting on a nest. Then she reached one hand out toward the hooks that held the bridles and reins, got a good grip then pulled herself into a standing position. She stepped from the bucket to the benchtop. "Ta Da! This is my stage." She exclaimed. Nessa laughed and pulled the carrot bucket a few

feet away from the bench. She sat on it and said"
OK, I am your audience, show me something great!

Stacee pulled the reins off the hook and connected the two together. Then she put them over her neck like a scarf. She began to dance as she twirled the reins in circles with each hand. Circle on the right, circle on the left, then both at the same time. She danced about the bench making her fancy foot work glide past and over the brushes, sponges and leather cleaner. Her animated moves brought her to the grain bucket so she leapt over it and landed on one foot balancing the other out straight. She had her arms stretched out using the reins to keep her balance. "I am on top of a horse. I am in the county rodeo show." Holding the pose, she slowly bent her knee up and down imitating the movement of the horse galloping. "See, I'm riding" She turned her head to look as Nessa and lost her balance. As she began to fall off the bench, head first, the twirling end of the reins flipped up in the air. They wrapped around one of the bridle hooks, pulling her by the hand, keeping her upper body from continuing toward the ground. She landed feet first with her right arm in the air still attached to the rein and hook. It looked like an Olympic gymnastics dismount. "I meant to do that" giggled Stacee. Nessa was on the ground rolling with laughter.

"Is it time to climb? Stacee asked Nessa. By now their eyes had adjusted to the lighting so the dark corners of the barn were not as scary. They walked over to the hayloft ladder. One rung at a time, Nessa ascended to the last rung and crawled across the hay. She turned around and looked down on Stacee. "Your turn!" She said.

Stacee climbed the ladder in the same fashion. Once in the hay they both stood up and looked around for anything new. The hay bales were stacked against the right wall with scatterings of opened bales around the loft. "Do you hear that?" Nessa said. Stacee tilted her head, the way you see a dog when it's master says "do you want a biscuit? She was listening intently and then heard it. In the darkness of the barn. where the roof meets the floor of the loft. they could hear the chirps of baby birds. "I bet those barn swallows have a nest up here." Said Stacee. They walked then squatted and eventually crawled, as the roofline got lower in the direction of the chirps. Sure enough, in the far corner was a small cup shaped nest attached to the wall with three baby swallows. The girls got close enough to see their heads popping up, beaks wide open waiting to be fed. Stacee began to reach in the direction of the nest as Nessa blurted "Don't touch them!" "What?" Asked Stacee. Nessa explained that a Mama bird won't come back to the nest if any human has touched the nest or the babies. "I bet they are hungry and their Mama can't come back to feed them because we are here. We should go. Let's look out the hayloft window and see if Francis is back." Said Nessa.

Greg had added a low window to the right hayloft door so the kids could view the pasture without opening them. It was an amazing view from the height of the barn. The green pasture below, lined with the pines and oaks and off in the distance the dark blue of the small pond. The family had already enjoyed a few loft picnics with the doors fully open to the beautiful view below.

The girls peered out the window and sure enough Francis could be seen. He was rolling in the grass just beyond the water trough. "Let's go" they said in unison.

By the time they got to the fence, Francis was there dancing for them. His usual tap-dance of excitement as he belted "Hee Haw Hee Haw"

The girls scaled the fence to the other side. Francis was in heaven as both girls pet his back and nose and scratched his velvety ears. He was hypnotized by the affection. "Should we walk to the sitting tree and eat our suckers?" Asked Nessa. "Sounds good to me" replied Stacee.

They walked across the green pasture, as Francis followed close behind. The sitting tree was just to the right of the royal maples that greeted her on her visits to the forest.

Standing at the base of the tree, Nessa reached out and patted Francis on his leg urging him to come close and said "Come on Francis, get close to the tree." He inched his way over, scratching up against the bark. "OK Francis, now lay down" she instructed, as she squatted down and patted the ground. Then she grabbed his left leg and gave it a couple tugs backward. Francis lifted his left leg and like a clumsy ox dropped his body to the ground. "Good job Francis" Nessa praised as she scratched his ears. Nessa and Stacee took turns using Francis's back as a step stool to get onto the tree's sitting branch.

It was the perfect "Chair in the air". The low hanging branch reached out perfectly straight. There was a space that had no bumps or baby branches. It was a smooth space for best friends to sit and listen to the songs of the birds accompanied by the wind.

Nessa and Stacee unwrapped their lollipops and up popped Francis. His head was level with the branch and there was just enough space, on the smooth spot, for him to rest his head. He lowered his chin on the branch between Nessa and Stacee and took turns looking up at each of them. Francis had a sweet tooth and his big brown eyes and long eyelashes were too hard to resist.

So the tongue lashing began on the blueberry deliciousness. One quick lick for Nessa. One long donkey-tongued lick for Francis. One short lick for Stacee another extended flavor stripping lick for Francis. The girls had to be fast to pull the lollipop away from Francis, near the end of his lick because he would try to get a nibble.

Both girls were generous with friends. Even if the friend was furry.

Stacee ended up staying for dinner. While eating a tater-tot casserole Greg shared his mechanical conquest on the Vet, Zach made fun of the girls and cracked his usual jokes, and the family enjoyed hearing Nessa and Stacee's adventures of the day.

CHAPTER TWELVE
Lonely Boy

The school days were hard for Francis, as his missed his best friend. He would spend hours staring at the house, waiting for Nessa to come out and play. When Steph came out the door, Francis would bray Hee Haw and as soon as he noticed it was not Nessa he stopped. Donkeys need companions and Francis was no exception.

Steph was sitting at the kitchen table, sipping a cup of coffee, when Greg came home. She smiled at him, stood up and gave him a hug and asked "how was your day?" He gave her a bigger hug, patted her on the rear and turned to hang up his coat and said "actually it was a fairly uneventful day" "That's good honey" replied Steph as she sat back down to her coffee.

"Greg, I have something to tell you. I think we may need to add a new family member and I was hoping…" As Steph attempted to finish, Greg's eyes widened as he abruptly turned his attention from the stack of mail in his hands to looking straight into Steps eyes. "Are we having another baby?" He asked with a mix of excitement and nervousness.

Steph began to laugh, standing up and shaking her head no and said, "no honey not a baby, another animal family member. Francis has gotten so lonely since school has been in session and Nessa doesn't have near as many hours to spend with him. I even think he is depressed. If we had another animal in the pasture, to keep him company and to play with, well I think it would help."

"What are you considering?" Replied Greg. "I don't know for sure but I thought we could ask around to find a compatible, easy care, friend for Francis." Steph said. Greg quickly agreed, "Sure honey, sounds like a good idea." After a moment of thinking he had another child to care for, getting another animal was an easy decision.

Over the next few weeks Greg and Steph did their homework to determine compatible animals for Francis. Then one day Jennifer came home from school with news.

"Mom, Mom!" Jen called out as she flew through the back door. "I'm upstairs" hollered Steph. Jen, with her long legs and slim runway model body, scaled the stairs, two steps at a time. She popped her head in Zach's room. Empty. Then next into Nessa's. Mom was making the beds and was wrestling a pillow case onto a pillow. "What's up sweetie?" Asked Step. "Well, I was talking to my friend, Amber and she said her brother raised a lamb for 4-H. Now they're moving into town and need to find it a home. We can have it for free. She said he is really smart and because he was raised with their dogs around, he is not afraid of other animals. Maybe he will think Francis is a big dog!"

"That sounds promising Jennifer, I'll let your Dad know and we will see what we can do" said Steph. "Cool" said Jennifer as she was making her way back down the stairs. She stopped about halfway and yelled back up the hall "His name is Skipper! Don't ya love it!

Greg and Steph agreed that a lamb would be an easy addition to the family and do well in the pasture. Greg and Steph took the truck to pick him up from Ambers folks while Grandma Hugg spent time with the kids. When they got to Ambers house they immediately saw a lamb in the driveway wearing a blue bandana. As they came up the driveway the lamb came running in their direction in the most peculiar way. It was as if the lamb was skipping. Steph and Greg looked at each other and cracked up laughing. "Now we know why they named him skipper" said Greg.

As they got out of the truck, skipper came over to Steph and nudged her hand with his nose. Steph practically melted right there.

After some exchange of gratitude, in both directions, and assurance that Ambers brother could visit Skipper anytime, they were on their way home with the newest family member.

Steph could see the kids and her Mom sitting on the porch anxiously waiting for them to get home. As they drove up the gravel road, the kids scattered off the porch like roaches when the lights go on.

The kids gathered around the truck to get a look at Francis's new friend. Greg pulled down the tailgate and hopped up into the bed of the truck. He untied Skipper and walked him over to the tailgate. Greg sat down then pulled skipper over his lap and tried to lower him to the ground but there was hardly a space to put him down with the kids and even Grandma wanting to get a first touch. They all helped lower Skipper to the gravel. "He is sooo cute" yelled Ally. "How precious" said Grandma Hugg. "Can he sleep in my room?" Asked Zach. "I can't wait for Francis to see him" said Nessa. "I am so glad Amber told us about him" Jen said as they started to give little Skipper some space.

Let's walk him over to the pasture and get him introduced to Francis. Suggested Greg. They all walked over like a heard of sheep. Or should one say, Lambs.

Francis had been near the watering trough and already on his way over having sighted Nessa. "Come on Francis. Come see your new friend" yelled Nessa.

Greg opened the gate and they all walked inside. Greg held the rope to keep skipper in place until the meeting was complete. Francis went straight to Nessa as usual. He got his ear scratch and hug. Steph suggested Nessa back away to let Skipper get closer. When Francis realized Skipper was there he put his muzzle in the air and brayed loudly Hee Haw Hee Haw, He then put his head down and pushed his nose into Skippers side. Skipper bumped his head into Francis belly. Greg un-hooked the rope. "Let's see what happens kids and they all backed away.

Skipper began to skip out into the pasture and Francis followed behind. Then Skipper turned around and headed straight at Francis and just like a bull fighter Francis moved just in time to avoid skippers hit. Francis took off faster than anyone had seen him move. Skipper followed and just when Skipper was about to catch up, Francis came to a grinding halt. Skipper ran smack dab into Francis's tail end. Skipper shook it off as Francis turned around. He actually looked as if he was smiling. Together they walked over to the water trough and drank side by side. After a few sips, skipper followed Francis over to the entire family that was sitting on the fence watching the new friendship begin.

Skipper ended up being just what Francis needed. He filled the void when Nessa was gone. While Skipper brought additional joy, he added a few problems to the Halstead family.

Skipper was smart. It didn't take long for him to figure out that he could fit between the top and bottom rung of the fence near the house. He liked the variety of the flowers and bushes that the yard gave him. This did not make Steph happy! The crazy thing was that he understood where he was supposed to be. If Greg saw he was out, he simply hollered "Skipper get back in the pasture" and he would crawl back under the fence where he belonged. On occasion a neighbor would drive by yelling "Greg, skipper is out again." And at times, just hearing the "tattle-tail" neighbor, sent Skipper back behind bars! You couldn't help but love him.

CHAPTER THIRTEEN

I'd Bank On It

The farm continued to welcome new members to the family. From a dog, a few cats, and even some hens to keep Petey the claw in line.

As the Halstead children grew older and everyone was in school, the days began to seem long for Steph. She was friends with one of the tellers at the First National Bank of Milaca on 2nd street and had shared that she may be looking for work. She told Steph that they were hiring.

After much discussion with Greg and the kids she decided to interview for the job. She had banked with them for years. As did all of her family. She knew their reputation. It was a family run bank that had been in business for over 100 years. They valued their customers and their employees. So after a successful interview, Steph found her home away from home. A perfect fit!

As the days, weeks and years past, Nessa's life became busier. She did her best to balance school, a part time job, church, movies, concerts and eventually a boy.

Even though she was growing up and had other interest, she never lost her love of the country life and her best friend Francis. It was Francis who helped her through the fights with her sisters, her sadness when Skipper died and eventually the break-up with her first boyfriend. Francis was there to listen and comfort. Nessa relished in their moments alone. It was with Francis that she was able to have her deepest thoughts. She always knew she would be OK.

A month after the break-up with her boyfriend, came a day that would change her life forever.

That morning she got up early to spend time with Francis before she drove to Princeton to attend the 9:15 service at New Life Church. She looked out her window to check the weather. The sun was just peeking its rays between the bases of the tree lined pasture. She could see Francis at the water trough. The warmth of his breath eased out his nostrils into the brisk morning air, sending plumes of frosty smoke like "Puff the magic dragon". She grabbed her winter jacket preparing for the chill, and quietly made her way downstairs as the family slept in.

As Nessa walked to the barn, her boots made a crunch with each step. Soon the snow would come and winter would be here in full force, thought Nessa.

She and Francis only did a short walk before heading to the barn. She brushed his coat and fed him a few carrots, while singing him the song she wrote so many years before. The air was fresh, her head was clear and Francis seemed happy. It was already a good day.

Back inside the warmth of the home, that she loved so much, she noticed the comforting smells as though she was breathing them in for the first time.

The subtle smell of dill, from Moms pickling spices, cinnamon from leftover apple pie and a pinch of earth from the boots and shoes that were kicked off under the hall tree. She sighed, smiled then pour herself some cereal.

After downing her light breakfast, she took a shower and got dressed. She was wearing black jeans, a white shirt with a white pullover sweater and a new pair of black leather boots. She caught a quick glance in the mirror. She looked and felt great.

Nessa tip-toed down the stairs to avoid clunking her heals on the oak floor boards. She was surprised to see that her mom was in the kitchen having her first cup of coffee.

"You must have snuck down here while I was in the shower" Said Nessa. "I'm on my way to church. I think I am going to have lunch with Stacee after. OK?" She asked, as she bent down and gave her Mom a kiss on the cheek. "Sure sweetie, see you later." Replied her mom.

She stood at the doorway of the church looking for Stacee when she felt a tap on her right shoulder. She turned to see no one. Of course Stacee had tapped her shoulder and ducked. By now she should have known. It was Stacee's usual trick, but she got her once again.

"Let's go sit" Said Nessa, a little anxious to get out of the aisle.

"Wait, I want you to meet someone" said Stacee as she grabbed her by the hand and began to pull her down the aisle to the right section of the pews.

Nessa objected "Stacee, who am I meeting? Slow down! I don't want to trip in my new boots"

Stacee stopped abruptly, causing Nessa to slam into her like bumper cars. Stacee pulled Nessa from behind her, facing a pew, where the stranger sat.

Stacee turned to Nessa and said." Nessa this is Johnny. Johnny this is Nessa."

Her friend was not introducing her to boy. No. He wasn't a boy. He was a man. He was a handsome young man. He was a Marine.

"He's on leave from Iraq. Said Stacee. Nessa was sure it must be his uniform that had her mesmerized. Tongue tied. Before she could get her lips to move, Johnny invited them to sit with him.

She was barely able to say a proper "hello, nice to meet you", before the service began.

They sat next to each other over the next hour, listening to the sermon, standing and singing praise songs and opening up the bible to follow scripture.

It wasn't his uniform that had her mesmerized. It was him. Everything about him. He was confident. He stood taller than his height. When he looked at her, while sharing the hymnal, he looked into her eyes. When he sang, he boasted the words as though they meant everything in the world to him.

Five months, later on a rainy April night, sitting on the porch, where Johnny grew up, Nessa would know that she meant everything in the world to him as he asked her to be his wife.

CHAPTER FOURTEEN

Francis Knew

The five months before their engagement was filled with long distance phone calls between Johnny and Nessa. First from Iraq and then The Marine Corps Base Camp Pendleton, California, where Jonny was then stationed. When he was on leave he would fly to Minnesota to spend every moment with Nessa. Many of these special moments were shared with Francis. Walks on the farm always included the fluffy tag along.

The first time Francis met Johnny, Nessa knew that Johnny was like no other. In the past Francis wouldn't let anyone else touch Nessa when he was near. Even her Dad, Greg, got a nudge-away when he came close to the two of them. Her previous boyfriend experienced a push into the pond when they were walking hand in hand one afternoon. But it was different with Johnny. Somehow Francis knew.

The first time he held her hand, while walking in the pasture, Nessa warned Johnny "be careful he will probably nudge you good to get you away from me.

Johnny held her hand tight and as Francis neared them Johnny put his arms around Nessa's waist and kept his eyes gazing into hers. "Nessa, he whispered, "kiss me". Nessa trusted him. She looked into his Caribbean blue eyes and for a moment forgot Francis was even there.

The kiss was slow and sweet. She felt her heart fill with warmth and joy and began to get lost in is embrace when she felt a wet warmth on her cheek. So did Johnny. Francis was giving them both a big, fat, wet donkey lick. Francis never did challenged Johnny.

After the engagement there were many details that needed planning. Picking a date and location for the wedding. Shopping for a wedding gown and bridesmaid dresses. Of course her sisters would be bridesmaids and Zach a groomsman. Eventually there would be a temporary move to California.

Even though life was busy, Nessa did everything she could to include Francis because he was not going to be able to come to California.

Steph and Greg agreed that Francis could stay at the Farm where he grew up and would probably need a friend to fill the void that Skipper left especially now that Nessa would be leaving. So Nessa and her folks sought out a friend for Francis.

CHAPTER FIFTEEN

Pen Pals

A week before the wedding Johnny called Nessa with news that his folks found a horse. Their friend Adam and his family, were being relocated to New York city for work. They had purchased a horse for their daughter, Sami Mae, and she had been riding Rita, a beautiful dark brown mare, for the past two years. He said she was heartbroken that they couldn't take her with them to the city. So they were willing to provide all medical needs and food if Rita could stay on the farm with them in hopes that one day they would move back. It sounded like a great arrangement if Francis agreed.

The next day Adam and his wife Melissa arrived at the farm pulling Rita in a trailer. Their kids Sami Mae and Braxton came along to meet Francis.

Nessa and Johnny met them in the yard. Rita was beautiful. Her coat was dark brown and shiny.

She had black stockings that blended to brown just past her thighs and a white wavy stripe from her forehead to her nose. She stood tall and proud as though she knew she was beautiful. Nessa wondered if she would shun Francis being that he was a simple animal. His fluffy fur was often half shed for much of the season. His ears were long and his mouth a bit of a wrinkle. He was damn cute but not handsome like a stallion.

Sami Mae backed Rita out of the trailer with the confidence of a cowboy. This little cowgirl was as petit as they come with twirling locks of brown and gold sun painted hair. She tugged the reins and led Rita away from the trailer straight toward the pasture without direction from anyone.

"She is pretty independent" said her Father Adam. "Knowing that she can come visit Rita is what is keeping her going" said her Mother Melissa.

Braxton ran after Sami Mae. He was a bit of a protective older brother and he wanted to be sure she would be OK.

Greg and Steph came out of the house to join in the introduction of Francis and Rita. Everyone stood back as Sami Mae walked her closer to the fence.

Francis was beyond the trees so Nessa gave her well-honed lips a whistle and then hollered "Francis come on boy" He popped out of the tree line with a bit of a kick in his gate. It was as though he was channeling Skipper. Maybe he was trying to impress Rita. Either way it was hilarious.

Rita saw Francis and began to whinny. Then Francis bayed "Hee Haw" "Hee Haw" and continued to come closer, faster. Nessa hopped on the fence as Francis got near. He stretched his head as far as he could over the fence in Rita's direction.

"Go ahead and bring Rita closer" Nessa told Sami Mae.

Rita began to reach her head toward Francis. Their muzzles met in what looked like numerous Eskimo kisses.

"Well, Sami Mae," said Nessa, should we put Rita in the pasture with Francis?" Sami Mae had a smile so big and sweet as she nodded her head up and down.

Nessa opened the gate and walked in with Sami Mae and Rita. Francis rubbed his belly against her side. He was a few hands smaller but his ears nearly came the same height as hers. "What do you think Sami Mae? Can we tuck the reins and let her run? Again she nodded.

Nessa helped her secure the reins and then said "Go on Francis show her the yard. GO!" Off went Francis and Rita followed. Rita quickly past Francis and headed straight to the tree line and when she got there she stopped. She turned back toward Francis and ran full speed straight in his direction. He was stopped in his tracks staring like a statue in her direction. "You better move Francis" Nessa said under her breath.

Just before a direct hit head-on, Francis gave a kick and a hop out of her way and ran faster than anyone had seen for some time. He turned back to see if she was following and she was. They were playing tag.

Nessa wondered how Sami Mae, a sweet little animal lover, much like herself, was going to survive in the city without her four-legged friend. She decided they would do it together. She shared with Sami Mae that she too was moving to the city and had to leave Francis behind. They agreed to become pen pals

CHAPTER SIXTEEN

Time Flies

The wedding was magical. Everyone that Nessa loved was there to see her begin a wonderful life with the man that cherished every good-hearted, animal-loving, bone in her body. God had certainly brought them together.

As most couples say about their wedding day; it went by in a heartbeat. Nessa said she remembers shaking hands at the receiving line and then suddenly the last dance was over.

They spent their honeymoon driving to California and moving into a condo near the base. It was close to the beach and walking distance to stores and the local bus. Johnny had already familiarized himself with most of the area but it was all new to Nessa. Everything was new to Nessa.

The world seemed to move so much faster on the west coast. The freeways had 4 to 6 lanes. The streets around their condo had two going each way. Fortunately, she convinced Johnny that she didn't need a car and could make her way around by bus or trolley. She would avoid driving on the roads at all cost. She wished she had Francis to ride.

Nessa did her homework to learn the bus schedules and how to connect to the trolley. She wasn't much of a shopper so the need to go anywhere without Johnny wasn't a big issue.

Nessa called her Mom daily. Dad was doing fine and working a lot out of town. Jennifer and her boyfriend Tony got engaged and Aly was dating a guy named Kevin that Mom said they really like.

Francis seemed to be depressed even with Rita to keep him company. Steph even brought her cell phone to Francis to see if he would recognize Nessa's voice. His ears seem to perk up as Nessa said his name but he kept looking around for her. It was heartbreaking for Nessa to think of him being so lonely.

Johnny and Nessa kept busy with week-end B-B-Qs, trips to the Zoo and Sundays at a local church they found. Nessa met some really nice military wives. She went for walks with one of the girls and had coffee with another. She did her best to fit in.

The first time she agreed to go with a group of the girls for an afternoon to get their nails done and have lunch, she came home holding back tears. They started the day by driving down the coast to the Fashion Valley mall. Almost 50 miles on 4 and 6 lane freeways with girls who talked more than they looked at the road. Nessa's knuckles were white from gripping the door handle so tightly.

The first stop was a sushi restaurant. She had tried to politely suggest something else but wasn't convincing. Natasha, the girl who drove, said it was "the bomb!

Nessa examined the menu. The prices were more than she expected. Even though Johnny had given her $30.00 Nessa didn't want to spend it all because they were trying to save to buy a farm when they returned to Minnesota. She had even called ahead of time to see how much a pedicure and manicure would cost so she could budget her day.

She looked for something simple. Even though there were explanations next to each Japanese word, it was all so weird. Anago (sea eel), Hamachi (tuna), Uni (Gonad of Sea urchin)

Nessa knew what a gonad was. She had been on Grandpa Hugg's farm often and learned how they remove them from the male pigs. Yuck! There was no way she was going to eat a raw gonad even if it came from a sea urchin.

She decided on an all-vegetable roll. The seaweed was kind of fishy but she managed to wash it down with the lemon water.

After lunch they strolled the two story outdoor mall. Minnesota didn't have malls like this because of the snow. There were 3 huge fountains and small vending carts set up throughout the mall. The girls continued from store to store looking at purses and shoes. "I could buy Francis a new saddle for the price of one pair of shoes" Nessa thought to herself. Did these girls really spend that kind of money on such things? Angeline, a tiny auburn spitfire, eventually did buy a pair of white Dolce Gabbana platform heals. Even though they were on sale they were over $300. Nessa couldn't imagine where she would ever where such shoes, especially because she would need a walker to keep from falling off of them.

None of the other girls bought the pricey purses or shoes but did fill their bags with make up from Sephora and the MAC counter at Macy's.

Their final destination was at Happy Nails. Natasha had made appointments for the manicures and pedicures. This too would be a first. Nessa did have her fingernails done for her wedding but had refused to have a stranger touch her feet. She was a boots kind of girl most of the year and just hated even seeing her feet. Now here she was in "barefoot" California. It was time to fit in.

Once inside the nail spa the world changed. There were women in reclining massage chairs reading books, watching TV and talking to each other while getting their nails done. The employees, doing their nails, spoke fast and foreign to each other. They seemed to be yelling at one another.

One lady, filing a woman's nails, yelled "May I hep you?" Natasha told her that they all had appointments for Mani-pedis. Then the lady said "Piga colo" "Piga Colo" and motioned to their left. The girls, without hesitation complied as they walked over to a wall filled with nail polish. Nessa followed.

Each of them were palming the bottles, lifting them to the light and sharing their opinions. "Wow check out the sparkles. This one is Niiiice" said Taylinn, as she flipped the bottle in the air and almost hit a lady waiting near the window. Tay, as her friends called her, looked like she was ready for the runway. She was sophisticated in a youthful way. Her light brown hair was smoothed back into a classic French twist with strands of metallic glimmer weaved in. Her red, shiny cotton skirt was fitted and complemented the crisp white pleated blouse that was separated by a wide shiny black belt. She wore red, white and black argyle stockings that ended just above her knees. She was like Audrey Hepburn meets Gwen Stephani. She was a sweet girl and boy did she eat a LOT of Sushi for a girl her size.

"Sit next to me" Taylinn told Nessa after one of the employees started directing each of the girls to a chair. "OK" replied Nessa happy she was invited to do so.

Nessa watched what the other girls did trying to follow suit.

✓ Put the nail polish on the little table that held the supplies.

✓ Sit in the chair.

✓ Hang your purse.

✓ Take off your shoes.

✓ Put your feet in the water.

"Ouch" blurted Nessa as she hung her feet above the tub of scalding water that had just turned them to a tomato shade of red. She apparently missed the "toe in first" step of checking the water first before plunging in both feet. "It too hot?" asked the lady, letting some water out and adding more cold before Nessa could answer.

Nessa checked the water first this time, then slowly added her feet to the bubbling water. She was just gaining a bit of comfort, in the oversized massage chair, when the lady shoved a plastic covered menu in her face and said "What you want?" She looked at the other girls who were already in conversation and answered "Manicure and Pedicure please" "You want cawus wemoved? You want wax?" The lady asked. "Uh? Well, um, no thank you!" Said Nessa unsure of what she was saying no to. "You want fower?" She continued. "Beg your pardon" said Nessa. "You want fower?" The woman repeated seeming to be irritated. So Nessa just said yes.

The next 40 minutes was excruciating for Nessa. She was already uncomfortable having a stranger touch her feet and then she had a Vietnamese drill sergeant giving her a pedicure. The lady roughly trimmed Nessa's cuticles like she was clipping coupons out of the Sunday paper.

When it was time to switch feet, she shoved one foot away and gabbed the other. As she scrubbed her feet with the pumice stone, she went at it like she was sanding an old board and even grinned when Nessa jumped as the stone came across the arch of her ticklish foot. The lady began slapping the bottom of her feet, as if spanking a misbehaved child, and Nessa nearly left her chair.

Nessa couldn't wait for it to be over. She had had enough of one woman assaulting her feet and the other holding her hands captive. Suddenly it was over. She was left in the chair with wads of paper between her toes and useless hands due to wet nails.

Hey Tay, what do we do now? Is she coming back? How long am I supposed to sit here? Tay giggled. "No silly, we go over to the drying chairs. You'll need to put your feet in too and they will give you some disposable flip flops." "Put my feet in what?" Asked Nessa.

Tay instructed her to carefully grab her purse and shoes and follow her to the front of the spa. There was a large square table with chairs around it. On top of the table was another smaller table with magazines on top and blue lights underneath. Tay showed her where to carefully place her hands and pushed the timer. Underneath the large table was another small table with another set of lights for her toenails.

When the lights went out it was time to pay. She went to the counter and the woman asked her who did her nails. She pointed to the chair where she had been tortured for nearly an hour. The front desk lady hollered something in Vietnamese to the woman who had done her nails then said" That will be $25.00" Nessa's heart skipped beat. She only had $22.00 left after paying $8.00 for her lunch. She had been told a Manicure and Pedicure was $18.00

"I was told it was $18.00 when I called last week." Replied Nessa. The lady told her that was a special that ended and the flower added $5.00 more. She was so flustered she dropped her purse while trying to search for any money she may have had in her bag.

Just then Natasha said "I have a coupon for $5.00 off, you can use it." Embarrassed, she thankfully took the coupon and apologized for the small tip.

The entire ride home she dreamed of being back on the farm, riding Francis through the tree lined pasture. He was always there for her bad days. Johnny was there for her too and cared deeply for Nessa and she trusted him with her life but sometimes she felt the need to be alone but not alone. That's what Francis gave her.

The country girl had a harder time in the concrete jungle than she had expected. The military friends were great but nothing was like home. She missed her family and she missed the farm and most of all she missed Francis.

CHAPTER SEVENTEEN

Facing Your Fears

Vanessa waded into the surf a little father this time. Getting in past her shins was a never before accomplished feat. Nessa was a good swimmer but the ocean was a powerful force she feared. She had seen the waves of Mille Lacs lake swell taller than her but the ocean harbored a different fright.

This time the waves were calling her in. Maybe it was the unusually calm day. The breeze was light and the sun was warm. The water temperature was at record highs.

She focused on her forward momentum pushing against the incoming waves. She was careful to steady herself against the current that could pull from the bottom, returning the waves to the vast ocean body.

Just then two boys on boogie boards skimmed past Nessa nearly knocking her off her feet, while other kids were making sand castles just feet from the waters brake. Vanessa arms flew wildly, to regain her balance, as she looked down and saw that her knees were gone. She had entered the ocean past the level of her shins. She was nearly thigh deep.

In her excitement to see if Johnny had noticed her amazing accomplishment she turned to wave at him and it was then she was pushed below the surface and pulled down. Suddenly the sounds of the world were muffled in the wet of the oceans grip. She was the laundry tumbling in the front loading machine. Pushed and thrown, tumbled and tossed. She kept reaching her arms for the safety of the sky and stretching her feet for traction on the sand but found neither. Tumbling in the bubbles, soon to become a lifeless floating memory, she pulled her knees to her chest and then pushed. The air hit her face as she gasped pushing the pillow off her head. It was but a nightmare.

She looked over and saw Johnny smiling at her. "I just had a horrible nightmare, I was wading into the ocean and looking for you when a wave hit me and I was drowning." She blurted. Johnny kept smiling at her. "What?" Nessa asked, irritated that he showed no compassion. "Today darling! Today!" Whispered Johnny. Nessa sat up in bed. "YES!" she grinned. It was moving day. Back to Minnesota. Back to family. Back to Francis.

CHAPTER EIGHTEEN

No Place Like Home

The 11 months had started slow but the last month seem to disappear like Grandma Halstead's rice crispy treats. In a few days they would be back. Back to Milaca Minnesota where the streets had two lanes, the food was cooked, the pace was slow, and the malls were indoors. Back home to her family and to Francis and Rita.

As they drove over the bridge, crossing the Rum River, and passed the "Welcome to Milaca" sign, Nessa began to cry. "are you OK honey?" Johnny asked. Nessa sniffled and said." I am soo happy to be home. I can't believe I missed this town so much"

They past the First National Bank of Milaca. Her Mom still worked there and had taken the day off to be home for Nessa's return. On the right was the Holiday superstore, where Grandma Hugg worked part time. Johnny took a turn, to go past the

Highway Café where just about everyone had all spent time eating burgers or pie. Nessa took a deep breath and said. "I'm ready to go home honey"

The truck percolated over the gravel road. Nessa could smell the sweetness of lilac and fresh cut grass. She couldn't believe she had been away for almost a year. They made the last of the turn in the road and she could see her house. Everything looked like it had been in a time capsule waiting for her return. The barn where she brushed Francis and played in the loft, the garage where Dad worked on his vet, the tire swing where so many children squealed with joy and the house where her family became county folk.

The back door flew open and out ran her Mother. Nessa was out of the truck before the wheels stopped rolling. She met her Mom with the biggest hug and as her Mom was twirling her around she heard it. Hee Haw, Hee Haw. She could hear Francis coming from beyond the tree. Nessa ran, jumped the fence and continued through the pasture. Francis breeched the trees and increased his gate. He was nearly in a gallop when her reached her. Hee Haw! Hee Haw! Hee Haw! Hee Haw! Francis continued as he danced in circles, rearing his front legs. "Hold still Francis! Calm down; you silly donkey, I want to hug you." Nessa pleaded. Francis nudged her with his nose, as she began to scratch his belly. He lowered his front legs in a bow to the fairy princess then rolled onto his back. Nessa got down on the ground, curled up and put her head on his belly. And she whispered.

Francis, Francis come and play.
Let's have lots of fun today,
We can walk or I can ride.
Carrots fuel your snail's-pace stride.
Francis, Francis you're my friend.
I'll be with you till the end.

"I'm home Francis. I'm home!"

Back row: Zach, Johnny, Tony Greg.
Second row: Ally, Nessa, Jennifer, Stephanie
Front row" Grandma Hugg and Grandpa Hugg

Johnny, Nessa and Ruby Mae

A special thanks to photographers: Candy Coughlin, Ally Novak, Emily Gerads, Jon Matthews, Vanessa Matthews and Christine Hugg.

EPILOG

Today Nessa(Vanessa) and Johnny Matthews live on their farm in central Minnesota. At the finish of this book, Francis turned 23 years. old.

Keeping Francis company, are four beautiful horses, Jack, Mina, Maverick and Presley. Francis keeps up with the horses as best he can and most of the time forgets he is a donkey.

There are two little Corgis, named Britches and Tucker, that visit the pasture often. The farm is also home for 9 chickens and a few nests of eggs soon to hatch.

The most important new friend for Francis is Nessa and Johnny's daughter Ruby Mae. Just a little over one-year-old, she is already a farm girl who loves her animals just like her Mommy and Daddy.

Greg works closer to home these days and Steph has been with the bank for 18 years.

Zach is still making people laugh, especially his Girlfriend Delany

Sister Jen married Tony, Sister Ally married Kevin and they each have a daughter, Daphne Shae and Bree La Rae. They are both close to Ruby Mae's age.

I think I hear a sequel!!

ACKNOWLEDMENTS

To the Hallstead, Hugg, and Matthews family I give my sincere gratitude for allowing me to tell their story. Especially Nessa for her willingness to be front and center in this book.

To my family Bob, Kyle, Natasha, Lance, Angeline Carter and Taylinn, for supporting my passion to write and for being my audience as ideas roll off my tongue.

To my 82-year-old Mother, who listened, as I read chapters aloud. For laughing and crying, which gave me hope that my words could convey, as I intended.

And to you, who have taken the time to read the words I put to paper.

I am grateful

Suzan

Made in the USA
Lexington, KY
14 August 2017